AIRPLANE FOLD

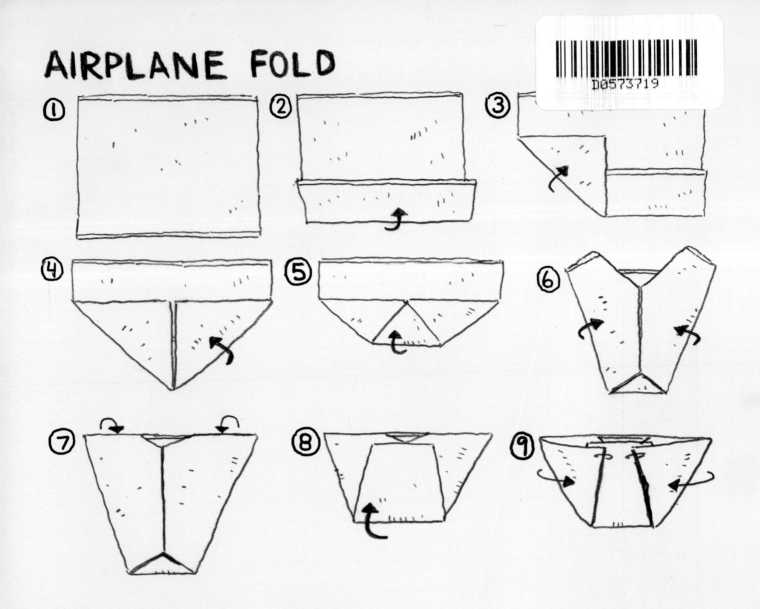

TRIANGLE FOLD

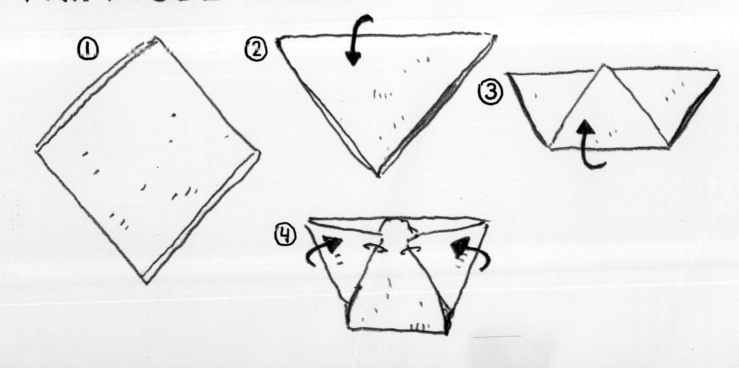

Dedicated to Roosevelt & Burgermeister;

Pequeño Smoocherton & Ladybug;

to Nece & Nene; and to Erica the Beautiful,

Jaybird & the memory of sweet Mandy —RM

For Alek and Kyle (and all the diaper-changing memories we had) —DS

ABOUT THIS BOOK

The illustrations for this book were done in color pencil, watercolor, and Adobe Photoshop. This book was edited by Megan Tingley and Esther Cajahuaringa, and designed by David Caplan and Prashansa Thapa. The production was supervised by Kimberly Stella, and the production editor was Annie McDonnell. The text was set in Danvetica, and the display type is hand lettered.

THE BABY-CHANGING STATION

WRITTEN BY
RHETT MILLER

ILLUSTRATED BY
DAN SANTAT

Megan Tingley Books
LITTLE, BROWN AND COMPANY
NEW YORK • BOSTON

People have names
And my name is James.
I'm a regular ten-year-old kid.
I always thought
I was nice but I'm not.
I feel bad 'bout this thing that I did.

See, it used to be
It was only me
And my dog and my dad and my mother.
Now there's this baby
Who's driving me CRAZY,
Joe, my brand-new brother.

Before Joe rolled in
I was the ten-
Year-old king of all I surveyed.
Now that he's here
It's perfectly clear
That I
Am in
The way.

Whenever he laughs
Or burps or claps
My parents lose their minds.
They think he's so cool
As he poops and he drools
Which he does ALL THE TIME.

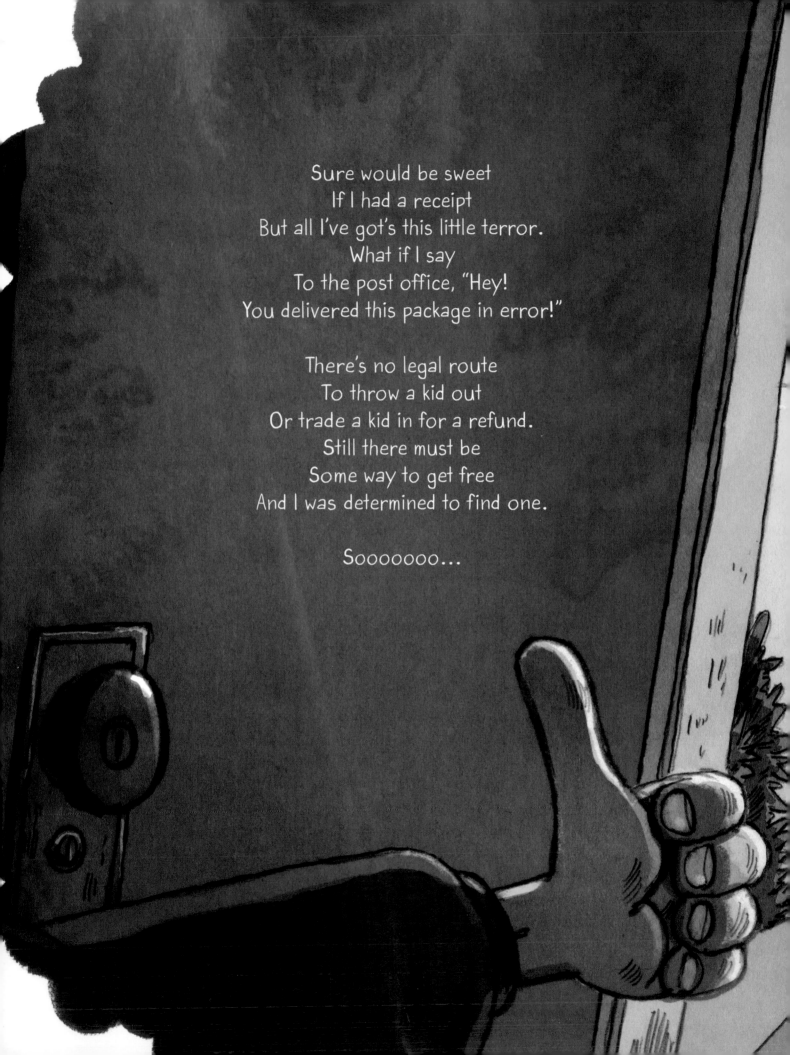

Sure would be sweet
If I had a receipt
But all I've got's this little terror.
What if I say
To the post office, "Hey!
You delivered this package in error!"

There's no legal route
To throw a kid out
Or trade a kid in for a refund.
Still there must be
Some way to get free
And I was determined to find one.

Soooooooo...

Thursdays are special.
That's our official
Family pizza night.
We drive in the van
To the Magical Pan
Where "There's Magic in Every Bite!"

My dad and my mom
They call it "the bomb"
Which apparently means it's yummy?
They eat and they eat
Then lean back in their seat
And groan and rub their tummy.

That's how they were
When little Joe stirred
And let out a tiny whimper.
We could all tell
By the subsequent smell
He'd loaded up his diaper.

Dad blinked his eyes
Like he was surprised
Or super exhausted maybe.
Mom said, "No way!
I've had him all day.
It's your turn to change the baby."

They stayed in their chairs
Glaring their glares.
My brother just sat there and stank.
They turned in their seats
And they both looked at me
And my ten-year-old stomach sank.

People have names
And my name is James
But normally Dad calls me J-Bone.
Tonight was not normal.
He sounded all formal.
"James, my son, this is a milestone.

"Your mother and I
Need assistance tonight
With your brother and his situation.
In that bathroom right there
To the left of your chair
There's a Baby-Changing Station.

"You may be a kid
But it's time that you did
Some diaper duty too."
That word made me snicker
But "Why not?" I figured.
I mean, what else could I do?

Sooooooo...

I carried Joe in
Through the door that said MEN
And found urinals, mirrors, and sinks.
This wouldn't be fun.
I thought, "Let's get this done.
For a little dude, he sure does stink."

The bathroom was vacant
And there was the changing
Table right there by the door.
I folded it down,
Spread some paper towels 'round
And readied myself for war.

What a disaster!
I moved a bit faster

Scraping and wiping and cleaning.
Next thing I knew
We were all through.
Joe was all powdered and beaming.

Then I noticed a screen
That I hadn't yet seen
And a big advertisement appeared.

I looked down at Joe
Who bothered me so
And I wondered if this was for real.
What will they say
If I trade him away?
Would their broken hearts ever heal?

As if reading my mind
Words appeared on the sign.

Before I could question
This crazy contention
A picture appeared on the screen.
Some weird-looking glasses
With high-tech attachments,
Camouflage, dark brown and green.

How fun would that be,
A brother and me,
At night sneaking 'round in the park?

I looked down at Joe.
Someday he'll grow
And we can play capture the flag.
We'll always win
But if I trade him in
What partner will I have?

The TV went blue
Then the words OPTION TWO
And a picture appeared on the screen.
Two six-string electric
Guitars looked fantastic
Like pointy, red rock star machines.

My dad's a rocker.
He's not into soccer
Or camping or flying a drone.
He likes Oasis,
The Kinks, the Van Halens,
Sly and the Family Stone.

More often than not,
Siblings who rock
Make the best bands, says my father.
My small bro, Joe,
Might someday grow
Into my musical partner.

He's already loud
And he whips up the crowd
Totally hogging the spotlight.
In music that's good, though,
Makes for a good show
A rock band with Joe might be tight!

The screen at the station
Then flashed FINAL OPTION
And showed a cool laboratory.
Folks in white coats
Holding beakers that smoked
Enough to make any mom worry.

Joe giggled and grunted
Like that's what he wanted.
He pointed and let out a squeal.

I looked in his eyes
And though he seemed wise
In a way that I'd never noticed
Little Joe may be
A dumb little baby
But it turns out he's into science.

A beeping sound harkened.
The TV screen darkened.
A countdown had started from ten.

MAKE YOUR CHOICE
NOW BEFORE TIME
RUNS OUT

THIS OFFER WON'T
HAPPEN AGAIN

The spy stuff specs were awesome.
The guitars were rockin'.
The chemistry kit was so rad.
And I could be rid
Of this dumb little kid
But the thought of that made me feel sad.

I want to see
What he grows up to be
When his infancy finally ends.
Though he's my nemesis
I see a world in which
He and I someday are friends.

Soooooooo...

The countdown reached one.
The magic was done.
The screen was suddenly black.
I rested my brother
Against my left shoulder
And started to carry him back.

People have names
And my name is James
And the best sound that I've ever heard
As I carried Joe out
He shouted it now.
My name was his very first word.

NEWSPAPER FOLD

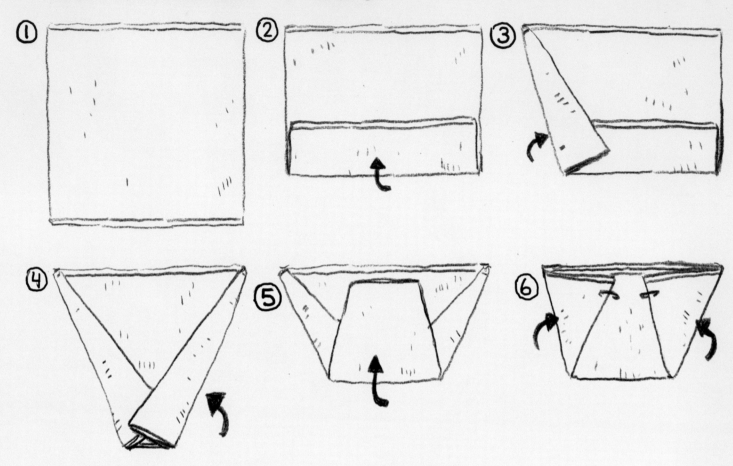

BIKINI FOLD

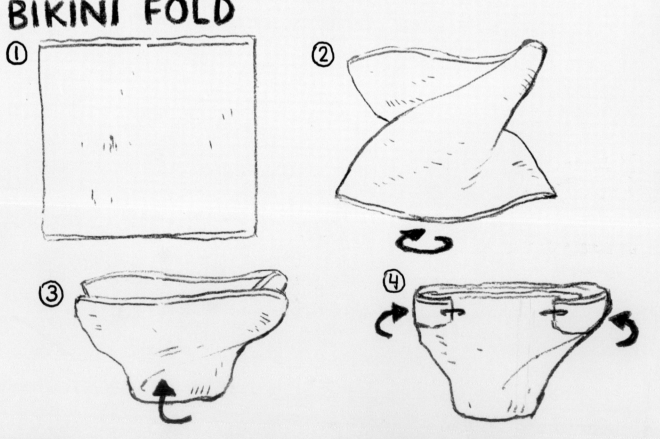